W9-CLI-017

REFERENCE LIBRARY ∗ HOUGHTON MIFFLIN CO. ∗ BOSTON.

Archive Collection

This book may not leave the Offices and it borrowed must be returned within 7 days

FAIR WEATHER

FAIR

Much warmer tonight
Monday partly cloudy
much warmer

FAIR

VOL 89 NO 119 Daily Leek & Sunday

Very Pistol Flares, Fired from Emory
Riddle Plane, Will signal Lindbergh's
Arrival at Destination, Delay or Disaster
Green If Flyer Wins Red If He Loses
White if He is Behind Schedule

TIMES-STAR TO FLASH

The Times-Star, aware of the
special interest manifested on the
first voyage of Charles Lindbergh to reach Paris in a non-
stop flight across the Atlantic
has arranged, through the coop-
eration of the Emory Riddle Company, commercial operator of
Lunken Airport, Station WSAI

and the Associated Press to signal day and night whether the
ship reaches its destination, is delayed or forced down

PLANE OFFICIALLY RE

Cable Company Re
... Flyer Approachim
Ireland

1:10 P.M. "IRISH TIME"

Irish Government An-
nounces that Dispatch is
official

LINDBERGH'S LOG

NEW YORK May 21

CHARLES LINDBERGH

Lindbergh is Model
of Clean-Cut Youth,
Associates Declare

NEW YORK May 21 AP

FLOO
VICTIM
FIRST T
BENEFI

CINCINNATI May (AP)

TIMES-STAR

AS THE ASSOCIATED PRESS DISPATCHES.

DAY, MAY 21, 1927   THIRTY-TWO PAGES   SINGLE COPY 2¢   BY CARRIER 12¢

HOME EDITION

EWS OF PARIS FLIGHT

*If he had completed double daylight to
Chicago run we see over city at
Flight to follow in the clad, city
seven thru what Saturday to do
layed thru WEB McClure until dark*

RTED OVER IRELAND

ef Justice Taft Says the Dog's a Failure, and No Wonder!

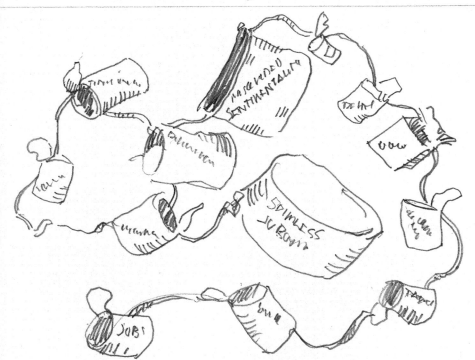

CINCINNATI AVIATOR WRECKS

PAPERBOY

BY **MARY KAY KROEGER** AND **LOUISE BORDEN**

• Illustrated by **TED LEWIN** •

CLARION BOOKS • NEW YORK

ACKNOWLEDGMENTS

The authors wish to thank Anne Shepherd and Laura Chace at the Cincinnati Historical Society,
and all good reading wishes to 4th grade students studying Cincinnati.

Clarion Books
a Houghton Mifflin Company imprint
215 Park Avenue South, New York, NY 10003
Text copyright © 1996 by Mary Kay Kroeger and Louise Borden
Illustrations copyright © 1996 by Ted Lewin.

The illustrations for this book were executed in watercolor on Strathmore Bristol.
The text was set in 16-point Amasis.

All rights reserved.

For information about permission to reproduce selections from this book,
write to Permissions, Houghton Mifflin Company,
215 Park Avenue South, New York, NY 10003.

www.houghtonmifflinbooks.com

Printed in the USA

Library of Congress Cataloging-in-Publication Data
Kroeger, Mary Kay.
Paperboy / by Mary Kay Kroeger and Louise Borden ; illustrated by Ted Lewin.
p. cm.
Summary: In Cincinnati in 1927, paperboy Willie Brinkman tries to sell extras on the
Dempsey-Tunney boxing match in his workingman's neighborhood.
ISBN 0-395-64482-8   PA ISBN 0-618-11142-5
[1. Newspaper carriers—Fiction. 2. Boxing—Fiction. 3. Loyalty—Fiction.]
I. Borden, Louise. II. Lewin, Ted, ill. III. Title. IV. Title: Paper boy.
PZ7.K9175Pap   1995
[E]—dc20   94-34246
CIP
AC
BVG 10 9 8 7 6 5 4 3 2

For our fathers, William G. Weich and William L. Walker
—M.K.K. and L.B.

To my father, Sidney
—T.L.

"*Extra! Extra! Read all about it!*
Two cents a copy!
Read the Cincinnati Times-Star!"

1927 was a great year to sell newspapers—
even on Willie Brinkman's small corner
at Hunt and Main.
Every day after school,
Willie's friends played "red ball, red ball"
in Erkenbrecher Alley.
But Willie had a job,
and his job was selling news.

Willie tied on his money apron
and waited with the other paperboys
while his boss, Mr. Schmidt,
counted out the *Times-Star* extras.
The latest news of the day was hot off the press.
Everyone in Cincinnati
was talking about the Dempsey-Tunney fight.
Everyone across the country
was talking about the biggest boxing match ever.

Everyone was asking, "Who will win?"
Everyone was asking, "Who will be
the next Heavyweight Champion of the World?"

"I'm for Tunney. I think he'll win!"
"Dempsey, for sure!"
"Jack Dempsey's my man."
"Tunney, hands down."

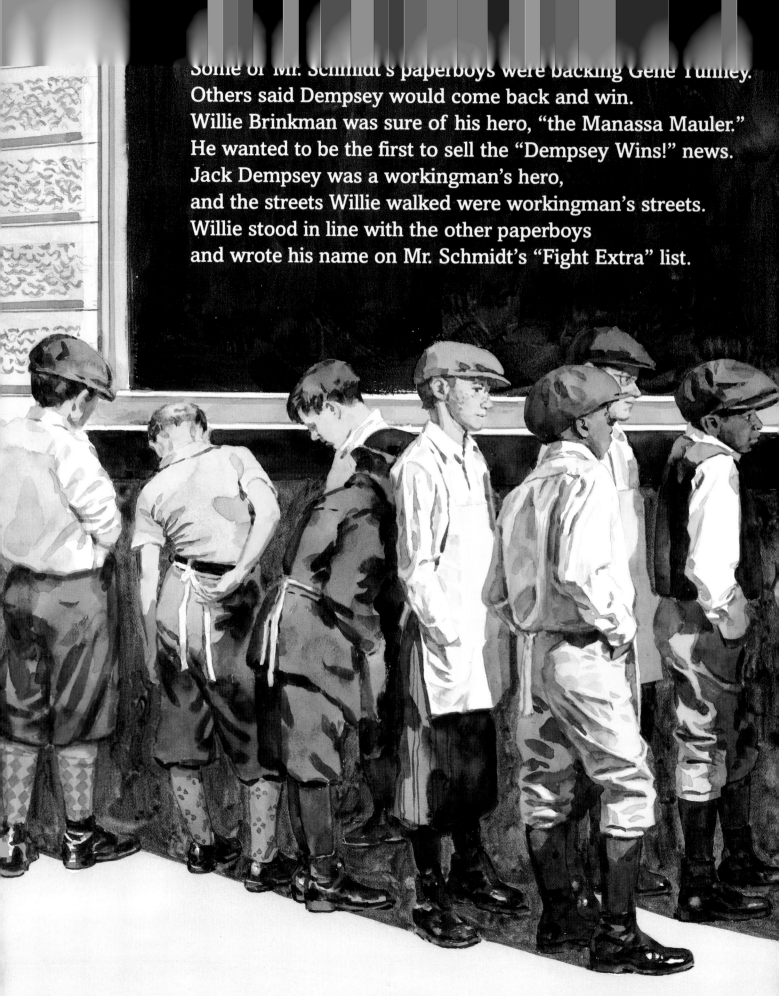

Some of Mr. Schmidt's paperboys were backing Gene Tunney.
Others said Dempsey would come back and win.
Willie Brinkman was sure of his hero, "the Manassa Mauler."
He wanted to be the first to sell the "Dempsey Wins!" news.
Jack Dempsey was a workingman's hero,
and the streets Willie walked were workingman's streets.
Willie stood in line with the other paperboys
and wrote his name on Mr. Schmidt's "Fight Extra" list.

9

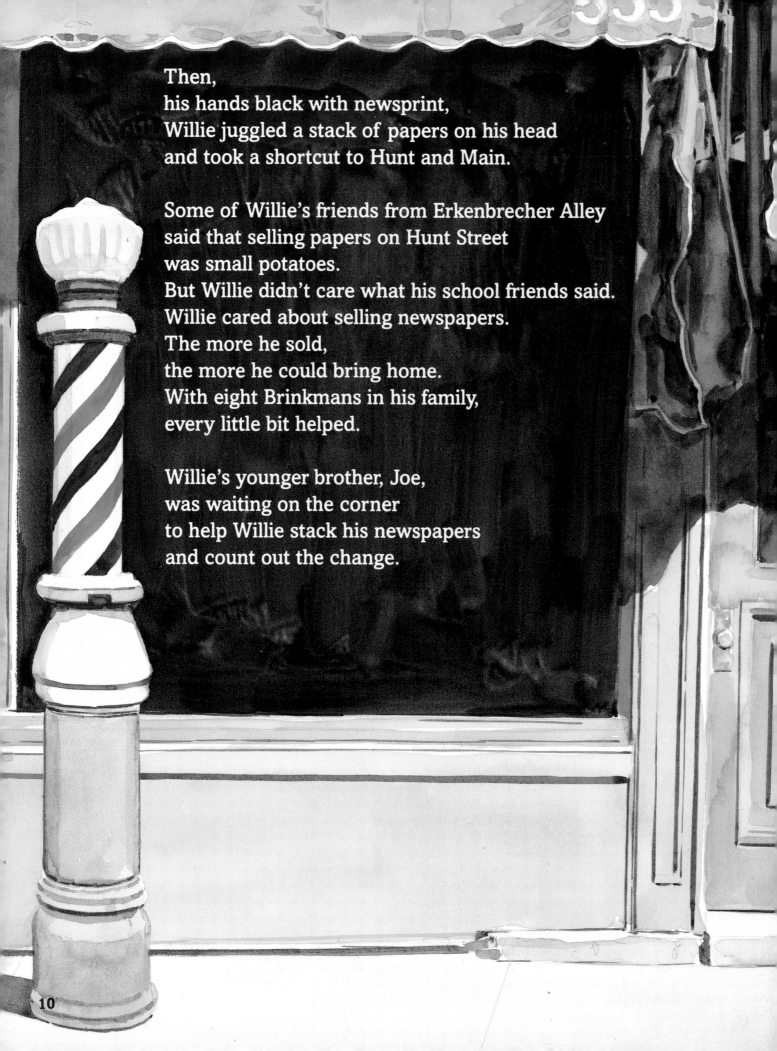

Then,
his hands black with newsprint,
Willie juggled a stack of papers on his head
and took a shortcut to Hunt and Main.

Some of Willie's friends from Erkenbrecher Alley
said that selling papers on Hunt Street
was small potatoes.
But Willie didn't care what his school friends said.
Willie cared about selling newspapers.
The more he sold,
the more he could bring home.
With eight Brinkmans in his family,
every little bit helped.

Willie's younger brother, Joe,
was waiting on the corner
to help Willie stack his newspapers
and count out the change.

Willie read all the headlines, front page to back.
Then he went to work, calling out the top stories.
That afternoon,
everyone wanted to know if Gene Tunney
thought he would win.
Everyone wanted to know if Jack Dempsey
was in tiptop shape.

"*Extra! Extra! Read all about it!*
Two cents a copy! Read the Times-Star!"
Joe stood right next to Willie
and echoed all his words.

What a day!
One hundred copies sold—
even on Willie's small-potatoes corner
at Hunt and Main.
Willie threw his cap in the air
and jingled the coins in his *Times-Star* apron.
One hundred newspapers at 2¢ each meant . . .
$1.17 for his boss, Mr. Schmidt,
and 83¢ for Willie's family to keep.

12

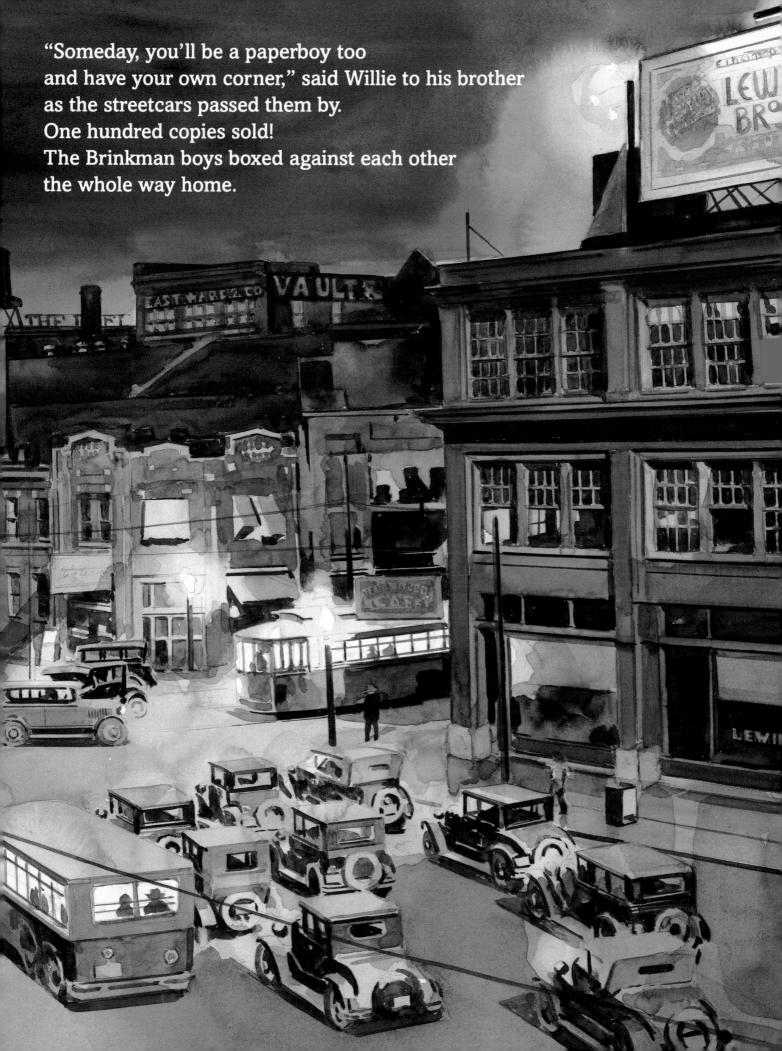

"Someday, you'll be a paperboy too
and have your own corner," said Willie to his brother
as the streetcars passed them by.
One hundred copies sold!
The Brinkman boys boxed against each other
the whole way home.

Willie handed the 83¢ to his mother just before supper.
Clink.
Clink.
Clink.
He listened as she dropped all those pennies and nickels
into the family mug on her kitchen shelf.
Willie Brinkman always stood a little taller
when he brought money home.

15

At supper,
Willie told his father about Mr. Schmidt's sign-up list.
"Please, Pop, let me sell the fight news tonight."
"You'll sell them in a hurry and come straight on home?
You'll be up in time for breakfast?
You won't oversleep for school?"
Willie crossed his fingers under his *Times-Star* apron.
He hoped he had just the right answers with all the right words.

Now get to that schoolwork," said Pop,
"so we can listen to the fight!"
All eight Brinkmans sat near Pop's wooden radio.
Miles away in Chicago, the fight of all fights had begun!
"Round one . . . Tunney is on his toes. . . ."

Willie closed his eyes.
He felt every punch.
He heard every shout.
"Round two . . . Tunney feints!"
"Tunney faints!" yelled Joe to his four sisters.
"No," said Willie. "That means he's faking a punch."
"Round four . . . Dempsey weaves in. . . ."
"Come on, Dempsey!" shouted all the Brinkman girls.
"Tunney takes one lightly on the body. . . ."
"Way to go, Dempsey!" Willie's mother was a fan.

Willie could almost see the boxers,
all slick with sweat, all shiny in the lights.
He could almost feel their big gloves,
all fat and punching, all smooth and fast.
And then in the seventh round—
only three more rounds to go . . .
"He's down! A big punch!
Tunney's down!
Dempsey's knocked Gene Tunney down!
Tunney is down for the count!"

Then . . .

"Jack Dempsey's still standing over Tunney.
He isn't going to a neutral corner."
"Get to a corner, Dempsey!" Willie shouted
to Pop's radio.
"Get to the right corner!"
Willie knew the referee couldn't start counting Tunney out
until Jack Dempsey went to a neutral corner in the ring.

One . . . two . . . three . . . four . . . five . . .
six . . . seven . . . eight . . . nine . . .
Tunney is on his feet, folks!
Gene Tunney is on his feet!"
Willie banged his fist on the table
and threw his cap on the floor.
Tunney'd had all those extra seconds to get up!
The fight should be over with a knockout!
Instead, the announcer's voice droned on:
"Round eight . . . Tunney's got his strength back. . . .
He's just opened a cut over Dempsey's eye."

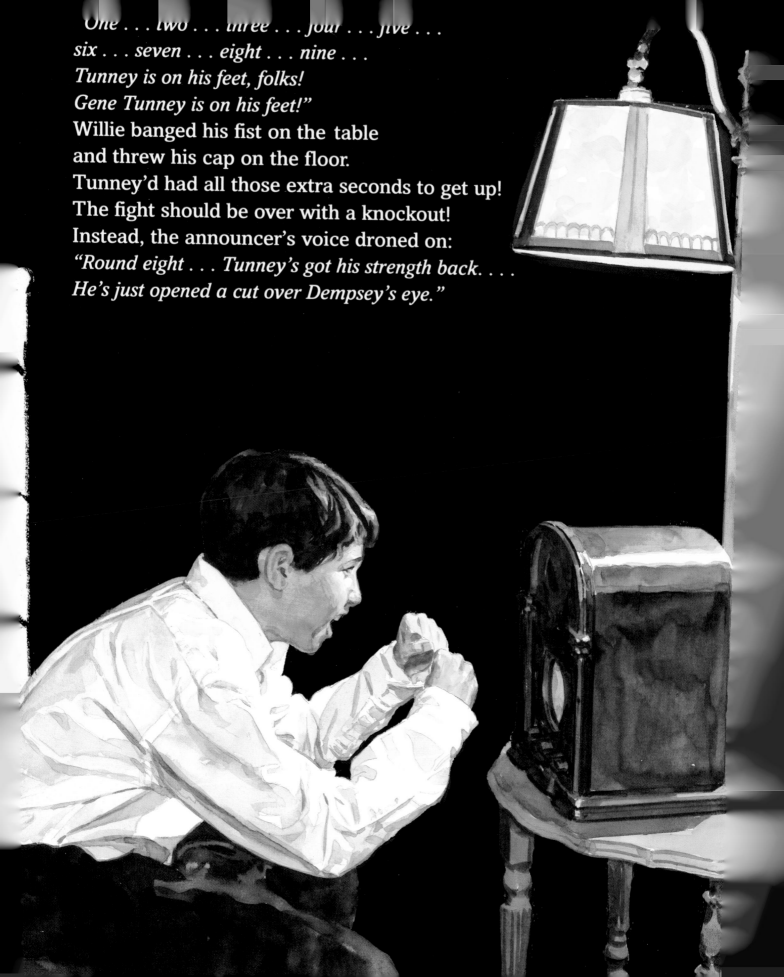

Come on, Dempsey." shouted Joe.
"Willie says you can win!"
But Willie was wrong.
Jack Dempsey was losing,
round by round.
Gene Tunney was the better boxer tonight.
"Round nine . . . Dempsey's staggering, folks. . . .
Three fast jabs to his face . . .
Another good round for Gentleman Gene.

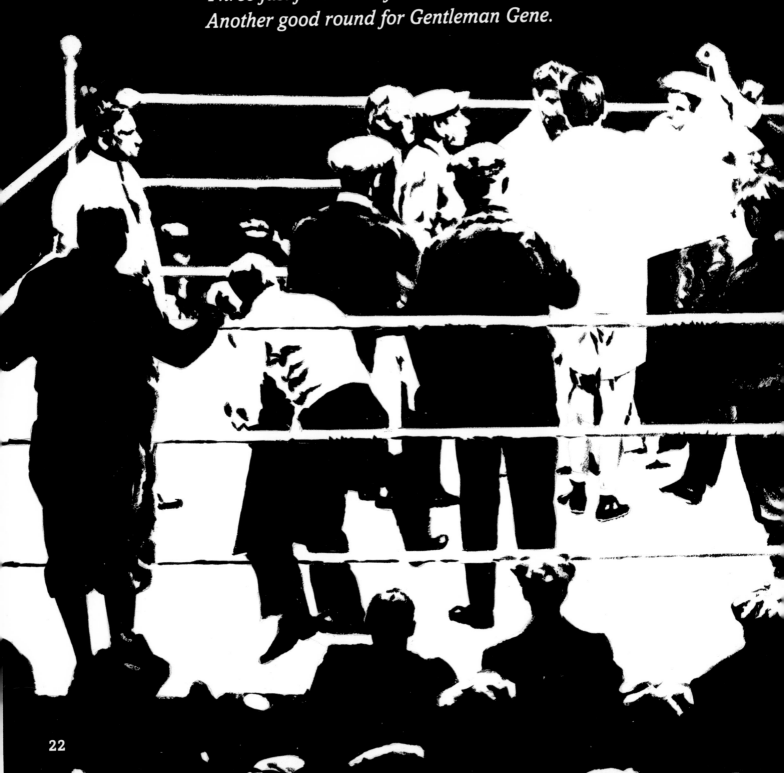

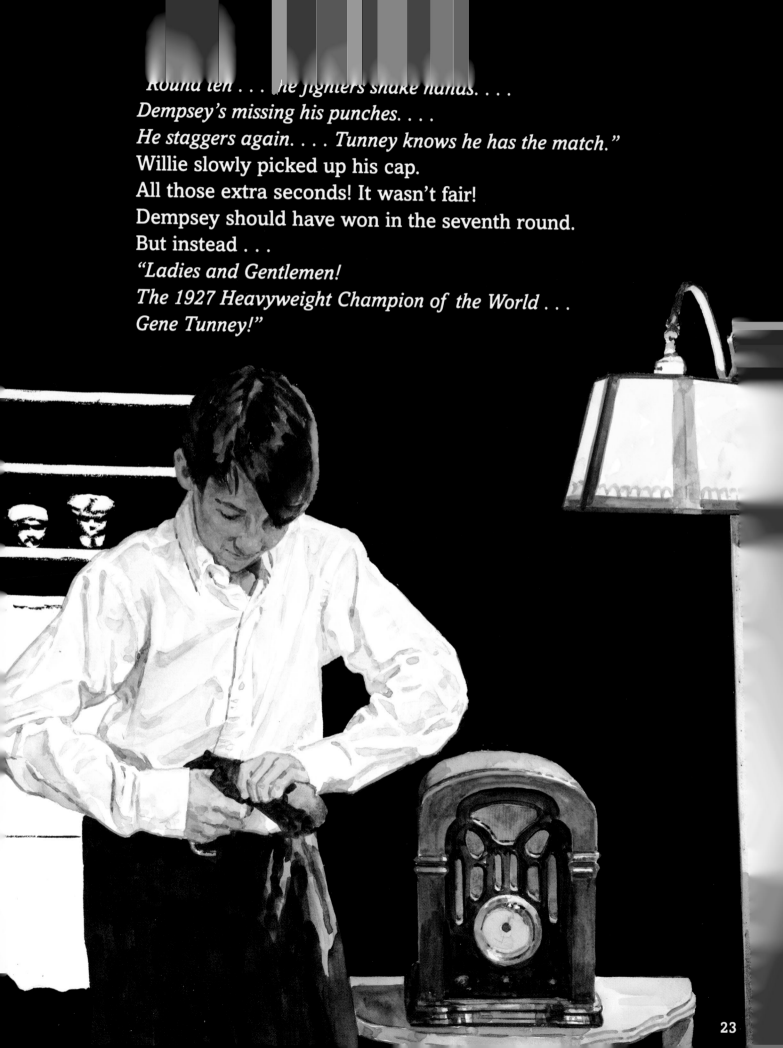

Round ten . . . The fighters shake hands. . . .
Dempsey's missing his punches. . . .
He staggers again. . . . Tunney knows he has the match."
Willie slowly picked up his cap.
All those extra seconds! It wasn't fair!
Dempsey should have won in the seventh round.
But instead . . .
"Ladies and Gentlemen!
The 1927 Heavyweight Champion of the World . . .
Gene Tunney!"

Willie Brinkman grabbed his money apron
and ran down the long, dark blocks
to the *Times-Star* building.
Mr. Schmidt was bundling papers, hot off the press.
He put his arm around Willie
and said in his deep boss's voice,
"You're the first boy here.
I just wish I had the news that you want to sell."

Willie hauled his "Fight Extra" papers through the streets
of his workingman's neighborhood.
The narrow brick houses were shuttered and dark.
"Extra! Extra! Read all about it!"
But no one wanted to read about Jack Dempsey's loss.
No one wanted to read about "the long count."
And a lot of Willie's neighbors didn't want to hear
that Gene Tunney was still the world champ.
Willie dragged his stack of unsold newspapers home
and dropped them in a heap on his front steps.
No coins tonight for the family mug.
No hundred copies sold . . . not even twenty-five.
Only "Lost Fight" news.

The next day after school,
Willie Brinkman wanted to join his friends in Erkenbrecher Alley.
He wanted to play "red ball, red ball" and race to tag the wall.
But then he remembered his hero,
Jack Dempsey.
A man who came back,
who tried a second time.
So Willie tied on his *Times-Star* apron
and waited with the other paperboys
while his boss, Mr. Schmidt,
counted out the day's news.

Everyone was still talking about "the long count."
Some were saying that Jack Dempsey should have won.
Mr. Schmidt counted off 225 papers for Willie.
More than twice the number of papers he'd ever sold in a day.
"I need a boy who shows up, and who works, win or lose.
I need a champ of a paperboy at Ninth and Main."

At Willie's busy new corner, everyone wanted the news.
All the lawyers from the courthouse in their pinstripe suits.
All the Second National bankers with their watches on their chains.
Even riders on the streetcars passing Willie by.
Willie was their paperboy.
And Willie knew the news.
"Extra! Extra! Read all about it!
Two cents a copy! Read the Times-Star!*"*

1927 was a great year to sell newspapers.
Especially on Willie Brinkman's corner—
at Ninth and Main.

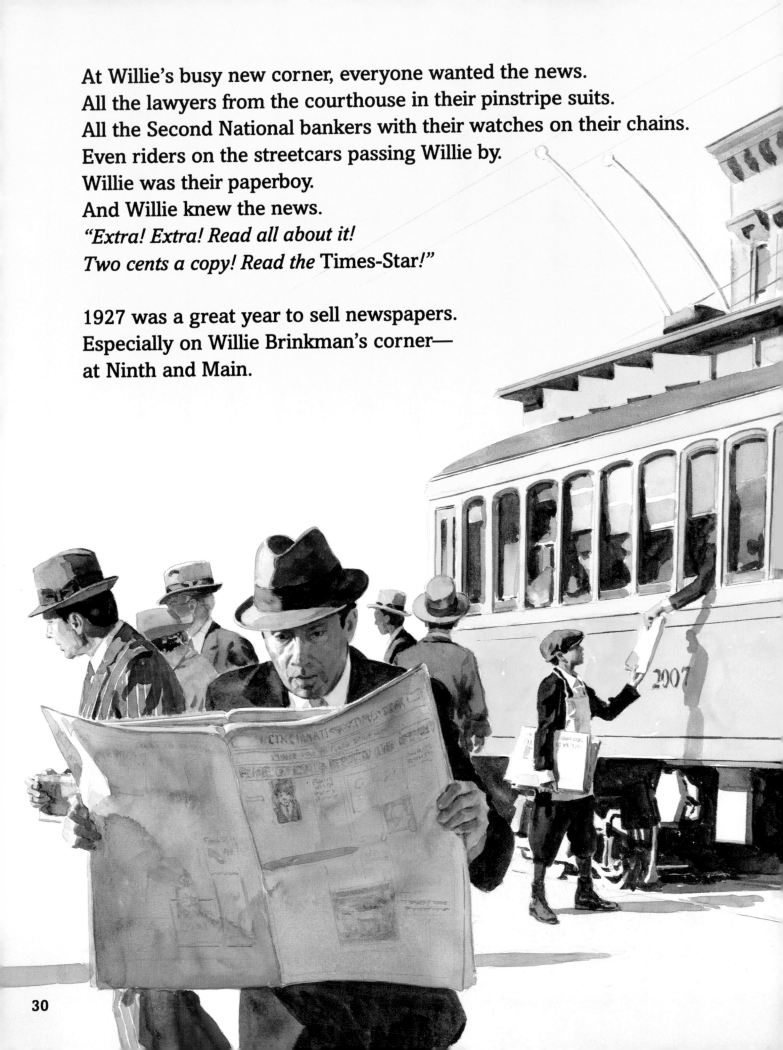

Authors' Note

Jack Dempsey was a famous boxer. His nickname was "the Manassa Mauler" because he was born and grew up in Manassa, Colorado. In 1919, when he was only twenty-four years old, he became the Heavyweight Champion of the World. He held this title until 1926, when he lost a match against another good boxer, Gene Tunney. James Joseph Tunney was born in 1898 in New York City. People called him "Gentleman Gene" because he read a lot of books. Now Gene Tunney was the Heavyweight Champion of the World.

Jack Dempsey wanted to win his title back. So a year later, on September 22, 1927, the two boxers went to Chicago and met in the ring at Soldier Field. During the seventh round, Dempsey knocked his opponent down but failed to go to a neutral corner, as agreed to before the match. This allowed Gene Tunney about six seconds more than the usual ten seconds to get back on his feet. Ever since, boxing fans have wondered about the famous "long count."

The title fight was all the more remarkable for being broadcast to listeners around the world. It was the first time such a radio hookup had been done for any sports event.

Jack Dempsey retired from the ring on March 4, 1928. Later he fought in many exhibition bouts. He was elected to the Boxing Hall of Fame in 1954. Jack Dempsey died in New York City on May 31, 1983.

Gene Tunney retired from the ring on July 28, 1928. He was elected to the Boxing Hall of Fame in 1955. Gene Tunney died in Greenwich, Connecticut, on November 7, 1978.

CINCINNATI

NO OTHER CINCINNATI AFTERNOON

VOL 17 NO 127 DAILY EXCEPT SUNDAY CINCINNATI

TITLE BOUT ECLIPSES A[...]

E.E. SPAFFORD IS ELECTED HEAD OF AMERICAN LEGION

New York City Man is Chosen
Vote unanimously

CLEMENCEAU HONORED

Choice of 1929 Convention
community Delayed.

NOT COMMITTED TO ANY FIELD FOR AIRPORT

Mighty Throngs Pack Streets
and Hotel Talking Fight

SOCIETY AND NOBILITY

Will Rub Elbows With Fringes
of Humanity at Soldiers' Field

By ALAN J GOULD

CHICAGO, September 22 – AP
– For the brief space of 34
minutes or less, Gene Tunney
and Jack Dempsey, fighting for
the heavyweight championship
in a ten round decision match,
tonight at Soldiers' Field, will
hold the eyes and ears of the
sporting world

GENE [...]

TIMES-STAR

HAS THE ASSOCIATED PRESS DISPATCHES

...AY SEPTEMBER 12, 1927   FORTY PAGES   ... 2c ... 12c

HOME EDITION

SPORT WORLD RECORDS

JACK DEMPSEY

COURT ORDERS MURDER CHARGE AGAINST POLICY

TWO AIRPLANES IN NON-STOP HOP OVER CONTINENT

NEW YORK ...

TWO SUSPECTS